# EVOLVE INTO A BETTER PERSON

M V TRYST

pencil

ISBN 978-93-5667-638-1
© M V TRYST 2023

Published in India 2023 by Pencil

*A brand of*
One Point Six Technologies Pvt. Ltd.
Unit no. 26, Ground Floor, Building A1,
Wadala Truck Terminal Road,
Near Post Office, Antop Hill, Mumbai - 400037
**E** connect@thepencilapp.com
**W** www.thepencilapp.com



DISCLAIMER: *The opinions expressed in this book are those of the authors and do not purport to reflect the views of the Publisher.*

# Author biography

M V Tryst is the author of 'Evolve Into A Better Person'. Tryst had a good experience in writing and is an eloquent speaker and writer.

Tryst is a student in Finance and Economics.

Tryst is a polyglot and is interested in learning history and cultures across the world.

Tryst loves to learn and share knowledge, and facts about the world through various sources in fictional, non-fictional, and poetic ways.

The book "Evolve Into A Better Person" is about 21 important aspects that a person should develop. Having developed all these aspects makes one super strong to face the world.

Apart from Health, one must focus on these 21 most important aspects to be holistically a better person. This book helps in achieving the best.

# CONTENTS

# Passion, Purpose & Ambition.

Passion, purpose, and ambition are three important elements that are often associated with achieving personal and professional success. While they are distinct concepts, they are all closely related and can work together to help individuals reach their full potential.

**Passion:**

Passion refers to a strong and intense enthusiasm or excitement for something. It is often said that when someone is passionate about something, it doesn't feel like work. Rather, it's something that they love to do, and they are willing to put in the time, effort, and energy to pursue it. Passion is a powerful motivator and can be a driving force behind personal and professional success.

Passion is a complex and multifaceted emotion that can arise from a wide range of experiences and activities. It can be ignited by an intense interest, a deep connection to a particular activity or subject, a sense of purpose or meaning, or a combination of these factors.

Passion is often associated with creativity, innovation, and entrepreneurship. People who are passionate about what they do are often more committed, engaged, and motivated to pursue their goals and dreams. Passion can also drive individuals to take risks, challenge themselves, and push beyond their limits.

However, passion can also be a double-edged sword. When taken to an extreme, it can lead to burnout, exhaustion, and a lack of balance in one's life. For this reason, it's important for individuals to cultivate a healthy relationship with their passion and find ways to integrate it into their daily lives in a sustainable and balanced way.

Passion can also evolve and change over time. What someone is passionate about in their youth may not be the same thing they are passionate about later in life. This evolution is natural and normal, and it's important for individuals to remain open to new experiences and opportunities that may ignite a new passion within them. It is a powerful force that can bring meaning, purpose, and fulfillment to one's life.

**Purpose:**
Purpose refers to the reason or motivation behind someone's actions or goals. It's about understanding why something is important and what impact it will have on one's life or the lives of others. Purpose gives direction and focus, and helps individuals to prioritize their time and energy towards things that truly matter to them.

Purpose refers to the reason why an individual exists or the reason behind their actions, decisions, and goals. It is a fundamental aspect of human nature, as it gives our lives direction, meaning, and a sense of fulfillment. Purpose is often described as a deep-seated sense of calling or mission, and it can manifest in a variety of ways depending on an individual's values, beliefs, and life experiences.

Discovering one's purpose is a process that can take time and introspection. It involves reflecting on one's values, interests, strengths, and weaknesses, as well as considering how one's unique skills and abilities can be used to make a positive impact on the world around them. Once an individual has identified their purpose, it can provide a sense of direction and motivation, helping them to make meaningful choices and pursue their goals with greater clarity and focus.

A strong sense of purpose has been linked to a range of positive outcomes, including greater resilience, higher levels of well-being, and increased engagement in one's work and personal life. It can also help individuals navigate difficult times and challenges, providing a sense of meaning and hope even in the face of adversity.

However, like passion, purpose can also be a source of stress and pressure when taken to an extreme. It's important to maintain a balanced approach to one's purpose, recognizing that it is a guiding force rather than an all-encompassing mandate. Discovering and pursuing one's purpose is a deeply personal and individual journey.

**Ambition:**
Ambition refers to the strong drive or desire to achieve something great or meaningful. It's about setting lofty goals, challenging oneself, and pushing beyond one's comfort zone. Ambition is fueled by passion and purpose,

and it can help individuals to stay motivated and focused on their long-term vision.

Ambition is the drive to achieve something, often in the context of career, personal development, or social status. It is a powerful motivator that can inspire individuals to take action, work hard, and strive for success. Ambition can take many forms, from a desire to climb the corporate ladder to a passion for creating something new and innovative.

Like passion and purpose, ambition can be a positive force in one's life, helping individuals to set and achieve meaningful goals and live a fulfilling life. Ambition can also be a source of inspiration and a way to push oneself beyond one's comfort zone and limitations.

However, ambition can also have negative consequences if not balanced with other aspects of life. An overemphasis on ambition can lead to burnout, stress, and a lack of balance in one's life. It can also cause individuals to prioritize their personal goals and aspirations over the needs and well-being of others, leading to a lack of empathy and compassion.

To cultivate a healthy relationship with ambition, it's important to maintain a balance between personal and professional goals, as well as to consider the impact of one's actions on others. This involves setting realistic goals and expectations, embracing failure as a natural part of the learning process, and cultivating a sense of gratitude and mindfulness to appreciate the present moment.

Ambition is a powerful force that can drive individuals to achieve their dreams and make a positive impact on the world around them. By harnessing the power of ambition in a balanced and mindful way, individuals can achieve their goals and live a fulfilling and meaningful life.

When passion, purpose, and ambition are aligned, they can work together to create a powerful force for personal and professional success. However, it's important to note that passion, purpose, and ambition are not always easy to identify or pursue. Uncovering what drives and motivates us can take time, reflection, and self-discovery. Additionally, there may be obstacles or setbacks along the way that can challenge our passion, purpose, and ambition. It is important to move ahead with belief. For example, someone who is passionate about painting might have the purpose of sharing their talent with the world and inspiring others through their art. They might set an ambitious goal of becoming a world-renowned artist, and use their passion and purpose to drive them towards achieving that goal.

# Focus & Concentration

Focus and concentration are related but distinct concepts. Focus refers to the ability to direct one's attention and energy towards a particular task or objective, while concentration refers to the ability to sustain that attention over time and resist distractions or interruptions.

In order to achieve a high level of concentration, it's important to have strong focus in the first place. This means being able to set clear goals and priorities, identify potential distractions, and actively work to eliminate or minimize them.

Both focus and concentration are essential skills for success in many areas of life. By developing strategies for improving focus and concentration, individuals can optimize their performance, achieve their goals, and live a more fulfilling and satisfying life.

**Focus:**
Focus is the ability to concentrate one's attention and energy on a particular task, goal, or objective. It involves directing one's thoughts and actions towards a specific aim, and avoiding distractions or interruptions that might impede progress towards that aim.

Having strong focus is essential for success in many areas of life, including work, school, sports, and personal development. Without focus, individuals may struggle to complete tasks or achieve their goals, leading to feelings of frustration, stress, and dissatisfaction.

There are many factors that can impact an individual's ability to focus, including external distractions, internal thoughts and emotions, physical fatigue, and mental exhaustion. In order to cultivate strong focus, it's important to develop strategies for managing these factors and optimizing one's environment for productivity and concentration.

Some strategies for improving focus include setting clear goals and priorities, breaking tasks into smaller, manageable pieces, minimizing distractions (such as turning off notifications or working in a quiet environment), taking regular breaks to rest and recharge, and practicing mindfulness techniques to manage internal thoughts and emotions.

Focus is a valuable skill that can help individuals achieve their goals and succeed in their personal and professional lives. It can be achieved by developing strategies for managing distractions, improving concentration, and staying motivated.

**Concentration:**

Concentration refers to the ability to sustain one's attention on a specific task or object over a period of time, despite the presence of distractions or interruptions. It is a cognitive process that requires active effort and focus, and is critical for success in many areas of life, including work, school, sports, and personal development.

Concentration is essential for achieving goals and completing tasks efficiently and effectively. Without the ability to concentrate, individuals may struggle to maintain focus, get easily distracted, and find it difficult to stay on task for extended periods of time. This can lead to feelings of frustration, stress, and low productivity.

There are many strategies that can be used to improve concentration, such as setting clear goals and priorities, breaking tasks into smaller, manageable pieces, minimizing distractions, taking regular breaks to rest and recharge, and practicing mindfulness techniques to manage internal thoughts and emotions.

In addition, it's important to optimize the environment for concentration. This may involve working in a quiet, well-lit space, minimizing noise and interruptions, and using tools such as noise-cancelling headphones or time-management apps to help stay focused and on task.

Concentration is a valuable skill that can be developed and improved with practice and effort. By identifying and minimizing distractions, setting clear goals, and developing habits and routines that promote sustained attention, individuals can improve their concentration and optimize their performance in all areas of life.

Focus and concentration are closely aligned and interdependent concepts. In order to achieve a high level of concentration, it's important to have strong focus in the first place. This means being able to direct one's attention and energy towards a particular task or objective.

Once focus is established, concentration requires ongoing effort to maintain. This may involve developing strategies for managing distractions and staying on task, as well as building the mental and physical stamina needed to sustain attention over time.

In order to align focus and concentration effectively, it's important to set clear goals and priorities, identify potential distractions, and actively work to eliminate or minimize them. This may involve developing specific techniques or practices for managing distractions and staying focused, such as setting regular intervals for checking email or social media, using noise-cancelling headphones to block out external noise, or practicing mindfulness meditation to cultivate greater mental clarity and focus.

In addition, it's important to create an environment that supports concentration, such as working in a quiet and well-lit space, minimizing interruptions, and using tools such as time-management apps or productivity software to help stay on track.

The alignment of focus and concentration is essential for achieving success and optimizing performance in all areas of life. By developing strong focus and concentration skills and using effective strategies for managing distractions and staying on task, individuals can achieve their goals and live a more fulfilling and satisfying life.

# Continuous Learning

Continuous learning refers to the ongoing process of acquiring new knowledge, skills, and insights throughout one's life. It involves a proactive approach towards learning and personal development, and it is an essential mindset for individuals who strive to be their best and achieve excellence in their chosen field or area of expertise.

Continuous learning:
Keeps you updated: In today's fast-paced world, knowledge and skills can become outdated quickly. Continuous learning helps you stay updated with the latest information, advancements, and trends in your field. It enables you to stay ahead of the curve and adapt to changes effectively, which is crucial for maintaining your competitive edge.

Enhances your capabilities: Continuous learning allows you to build and enhance your capabilities, including your knowledge, skills, and abilities. It helps you develop expertise in your field and hone your craft, making you better equipped to perform at your best and excel in your work or profession.

Fosters personal growth: Continuous learning promotes personal growth and development. It expands your horizons, exposes you to new ideas and perspectives, and challenges you to step out of your comfort zone. It encourages critical thinking, creativity, and problem-solving skills, which are valuable both in your professional life and your personal life.

Supports career advancement: Continuous learning is often linked to career advancement. It helps you acquire new skills and knowledge that can qualify you for new opportunities, promotions, or career transitions. It also demonstrates your commitment to self-improvement and professional growth, which can be attractive to employers and open up doors for career advancement.

Builds resilience and adaptability: Continuous learning cultivates resilience and adaptability, which are essential qualities for navigating the ever-changing dynamics of the modern world. It helps you develop a growth mindset and the ability to embrace change, learn from failures, and bounce back from setbacks.

Encourages innovation: Continuous learning fuels innovation by exposing you to new ideas, perspectives, and approaches. It encourages you to think critically, challenge existing assumptions, and come up with new solutions to problems. Innovation is a key driver of success in today's rapidly evolving world, and continuous learning provides the foundation for it.

It is vital to personal and professional growth. It equips you with the knowledge, skills, and capabilities to adapt, excel, and innovate in an ever-changing world, making it essential for those who strive to be the best in their field. Embracing a mindset of continuous learning can lead to improved performance, expanded opportunities, and enhanced personal and professional growth. So, it's important to prioritize continuous learning and make it a lifelong habit for ongoing success and excellence.

# Positive Attitude

A positive attitude is a mental outlook that reflects a constructive and optimistic perspective toward oneself, others, and the world. It involves maintaining a hopeful and positive mindset, despite challenges, setbacks, or adversity. A positive attitude is characterized by an optimistic and proactive approach to life, a belief in one's abilities, a willingness to learn and grow, and an overall positive demeanor in thoughts, words, and actions.

Improves Mental and Emotional Well-being: A positive attitude has been shown to have a direct impact on mental and emotional well-being. It helps reduce stress, anxiety, and depression and promotes a sense of happiness, contentment, and fulfillment. A positive attitude fosters resilience, allowing individuals to bounce back from setbacks and challenges with a greater sense of hope and determination.

Enhances Relationships: Positive attitude also plays a crucial role in building and maintaining healthy relationships. It helps in fostering positive interactions with others, promoting effective communication, and building trust and rapport. People with a positive attitude are more likely to be perceived as approachable, friendly, and empathetic, which can lead to stronger and more meaningful connections with others.

Increases Productivity and Success: A positive attitude is closely linked to increased productivity and success in various areas of life. It promotes a proactive and solution-oriented mindset, which helps individuals approach challenges with a can-do attitude and seek opportunities for growth and improvement. A positive attitude also encourages perseverance, resilience, and a willingness to take risks, which are essential traits for achieving success in any endeavor.

Better Physical Health: Research has shown that a positive attitude can positively impact physical health as well. Positive emotions and attitudes have been linked to better cardiovascular health, improved immune function, and reduced risk of chronic diseases. A positive attitude towards exercise, healthy eating, and self-care can also lead to better physical well-being.

Lifelong Learning and Growth: A positive attitude is closely associated with a growth mindset, which is a belief that abilities and intelligence can be developed through effort, learning, and practice. Embracing a positive attitude towards learning fosters a curiosity to explore new ideas, acquire new knowledge, and develop new skills. It encourages continuous learning and personal growth, which are essential for staying relevant and adaptable in today's fast-changing world.

Not having a positive attitude can lead to various problems, such as:

Low self-esteem: A negative attitude can cause a person to doubt their abilities and worth, which can result in low self-esteem.

Lack of motivation: Negative thoughts and beliefs can cause a person to feel unmotivated, leading to procrastination and lack of productivity.

Poor relationships: Negativity can be contagious, and people with a negative attitude may have trouble forming and maintaining healthy relationships.

Increased stress: A negative attitude can lead to increased stress levels and can make it harder for a person to cope with difficult situations.

Poor mental and physical health: Prolonged negativity can lead to mental and physical health problems, including depression, anxiety, and chronic illnesses.

Limited opportunities: A negative attitude can limit a person's opportunities in life, as they may be less likely to take risks or try new things.

Not having a positive attitude can hinder personal growth and success, making it important to work on developing a positive mindset.

A positive attitude is a key ingredient for being the best version of oneself. It promotes mental and emotional well-being, enhances relationships, increases productivity and success, improves physical health, and fosters lifelong learning and growth. Cultivating a positive attitude can lead to a more fulfilling and successful life, and it is a mindset that can be developed through conscious effort, self-reflection, and practice. Embracing a positive attitude can empower individuals to overcome challenges, achieve their goals, and lead happier and more fulfilling life. Maintaining a positive attitude is crucial for personal and professional success. So, always strive to cultivate a positive attitude in your thoughts, words, and actions, and you'll be well on your way to being the best version of yourself. Remember that a positive attitude is a choice, and it's never too late to start adopting one. So, go ahead and embrace a positive attitude, and watch how it can transform your life for the better.

# Resilience

Resilience refers to the ability to bounce back from setbacks, adapt to changing circumstances, and thrive in the face of adversity. It plays a critical role in transforming oneself into the best version possible.

Resilience helps you overcome obstacles: Life is full of challenges, and setbacks are inevitable. Resilience helps you navigate these challenges with grace and determination, rather than giving up or feeling defeated. With a resilient mindset, you are better able to overcome obstacles and emerge stronger on the other side.

Resilience fosters growth and learning: When faced with difficulties, resilient individuals see them as opportunities for growth and learning. They are not afraid to make mistakes and use setbacks as a chance to gain new insights and skills.

Resilience promotes mental and emotional well-being: Resilient individuals tend to have a more positive outlook on life, which can have a powerful impact on their mental and emotional well-being. They are better able to manage stress, cope with challenges, and maintain a sense of balance and perspective.

Resilience fuels success: Whether in personal or professional pursuits, resilience is often the key to success. Those who are resilient are better able to set and achieve goals, persevere in the face of challenges, and adapt to changing circumstances.

To build resilience, it's important to cultivate positive coping strategies, such as mindfulness, exercise, and social support. It's also important to develop a growth mindset, which involves seeing challenges as opportunities for growth and learning. By cultivating resilience, you can transform yourself into the best possible version and overcome any obstacle that comes your way.

Resilience helps build self-confidence: When you successfully overcome challenges and setbacks, it helps build self-confidence and self-esteem. This can have a positive impact on other areas of your life, such as your relationships and career.

Resilience fosters positive relationships: Resilient People tend to have stronger, more positive relationships. They are better able to communicate their needs, manage conflicts, and support others in their resilience journeys.

Resilience encourages creativity and innovation: When faced with obstacles, resilient individuals are more likely to think creatively and outside the box to find solutions. This can lead to innovation and new ways of thinking and doing things.

Resilience helps cultivate gratitude and optimism: Resilient individuals tend to have a more positive outlook on life, which can help cultivate gratitude and optimism. This can have a powerful impact on mental and emotional well-being, and may even contribute to physical health benefits.

Resilience is an essential quality for transforming yourself into the best possible version. By cultivating a resilient mindset and positive coping strategies, you can overcome challenges, foster growth, and learning, build self-confidence, cultivate positive relationships, encourage creativity and innovation, and cultivate gratitude and optimism.

# Adaptability

Adaptability refers to the ability of an individual or an organization to adjust to changing circumstances and environments. It is a valuable trait to have in both personal and professional life because the ability to adapt to new situations is crucial for success. Being adaptable means being open to new ideas, being flexible, and being able to adjust one's behavior or strategies to fit new circumstances.

Adaptability is important because change is inevitable, and being able to adapt can help individuals and organizations thrive. Adaptable individuals are better equipped to handle changes in their personal and professional lives, such as changes in the workplace, changes in relationships, or changes in their living situations. They are able to view challenges as opportunities for growth and learning and can approach new situations with a positive attitude.

Adaptability also plays a critical role in organizational success. Companies that are adaptable are better able to respond to changes in the market, changes in technology, or changes in consumer preferences. They are able to pivot quickly and efficiently and can stay ahead of their competitors.

To develop adaptability, individuals can practice being open to new ideas and experiences, cultivate a growth mindset, and learn to embrace change. It is important to be willing to take risks and try new things, even if they may not always be successful. Developing problem-solving skills and learning to be resourceful can also help build adaptability. It is important to remember that adaptability is not about being perfect, but rather about being willing to learn and grow from new experiences.

There are some ways that adaptability can play a role in success. They are:

Adapting to change: Change is an inevitable part of life, and those who can adapt to change are better equipped to thrive. Adaptable people are able to embrace change and find ways to make the most of new situations, rather than getting stuck in the past.

Staying relevant: In today's fast-paced world, skills and technologies become outdated quickly. Those who are adaptable are better able to stay up to date and relevant in their industry. This can lead to more opportunities for growth and advancement.

Problem-solving: Adaptable people are often skilled problem-solvers. They are able to analyze a situation and come up with creative solutions that may not have been obvious at first. This can be especially helpful in complex or rapidly changing environments.

Building relationships: Being adaptable can also help build stronger relationships. People who are adaptable are often more approachable and open to new ideas and perspectives. This can lead to more productive collaborations and partnerships.

Adaptability is important because life is unpredictable and situations are constantly changing. In order to thrive in different environments, it is necessary to be able to adjust one's behavior, thoughts, and actions accordingly. Those who are adaptable are more likely to succeed in their personal and professional lives because they are able to handle unexpected challenges and are more open to new opportunities.

Adaptability also allows individuals to become more versatile and expand their skill sets. By being open to learning and adapting to new situations, individuals are able to develop new ways of thinking and problem-solving, which can help them excel in their careers and personal lives.

In today's fast-paced and ever-changing world, adaptability is a crucial skill to have. It enables individuals to keep up with the latest developments and trends in their industries and to quickly adjust to changes in their environment. Being adaptable allows individuals to stay relevant and valuable in their fields, making them more employable and competitive in the job market.

# Perseverance

Perseverance is the ability to persist in the face of obstacles, setbacks, and challenges. It involves maintaining a strong and determined attitude in the pursuit of a goal, even when faced with difficulties and setbacks. Perseverance is a key trait for achieving success, as it allows individuals to push through challenges and achieve their objectives.

Perseverance can take many forms, from working long hours to overcome obstacles to staying focused on a goal even when faced with distractions. It requires a high degree of mental and emotional fortitude, as individuals must be able to push through pain, frustration, and doubt. In many cases, perseverance also requires creativity and flexibility, as individuals must be willing to adapt their approach as needed to overcome challenges.

One of the key benefits of perseverance is that it builds resilience. When individuals persist in the face of obstacles and setbacks, they develop a greater capacity to handle adversity and cope with stress. This resilience can be a valuable asset in all areas of life, from personal relationships to business ventures.

To develop perseverance, it is important to set clear goals and to maintain a positive attitude. It is also important to stay focused on the big picture and to maintain a sense of purpose and direction, even when faced with setbacks. Additionally, it can be helpful to break down goals into smaller, more manageable tasks, and to celebrate each milestone along the way.

Ultimately, perseverance is a mindset that can be developed through consistent effort and practice. By cultivating a strong sense of determination and resilience, individuals can push through challenges and achieve success in all areas of their lives.

Not developing perseverance can lead to several problems in both personal and professional life. Some of them are:

Giving up easily: Without perseverance, people tend to give up easily when faced with challenges or obstacles. They lack the motivation and determination to push through difficult times, which can lead to missed opportunities and unfulfilled potential.

Procrastination: Without perseverance, it is easy to fall into the trap of procrastination. People may delay taking action on important tasks or goals, which can result in missed deadlines, lost opportunities, and even failure.

Lack of discipline: Perseverance requires discipline, commitment, and consistency. Without it, people may struggle to maintain focus and stay on track, leading to inconsistency and lack of progress.

Inability to handle failure: Failure is an inevitable part of life, and without perseverance, people may struggle to handle it. They may become demotivated or discouraged, and give up on their goals altogether.

Low self-confidence: Not developing perseverance can also impact self-confidence. People may doubt their abilities and question whether they can achieve their goals, leading to a lack of confidence and self-esteem.

Overall, developing perseverance is crucial for success and personal growth. It allows individuals to overcome challenges, stay focused on their goals, and achieve their full potential.

Developing perseverance, or the ability to persist in the face of challenges and obstacles, can have numerous benefits in both personal and professional aspects of life. Some of the benefits of developing perseverance are:
Achievement of goals: Perseverance helps individuals to stay focused and determined in achieving their goals. It enables them to persist through setbacks and failures, and to keep moving forward towards their objectives.

Increased self-confidence: When individuals develop perseverance, they become more confident in their abilities to tackle difficult challenges. They learn to trust their own abilities, and to believe in themselves even when faced with setbacks or failures.

Better problem-solving skills: Perseverance requires individuals to think creatively and critically about solutions to problems. This leads to the development of better problem-solving skills and the ability to think outside the box.

Increased resilience: Perseverance helps individuals to develop resilience, or the ability to bounce back from setbacks and challenges. This enables them to handle stress and adversity with greater ease.

Improved motivation: When individuals have a strong sense of perseverance, they become more motivated to achieve their goals. They are more likely to work harder and longer to achieve success, and to stay focused on their objectives even in the face of distractions or competing priorities.

Ultimately, developing perseverance can lead to greater success and fulfillment in both personal and professional aspects of life.

# Creativity & Innovation

Creativity and innovation are two important concepts that are closely related to each other. Creativity is the ability to generate new and original ideas, while innovation is the process of turning those ideas into tangible products or services that provide value to customers.

**Creativity:**
Creativity is the ability to think outside of the box and come up with new and innovative ideas. It is a key skill in many fields, including art, design, engineering, business, and science. Creativity involves not just coming up with ideas but also bringing those ideas to life and implementing them in a practical way.

One of the biggest benefits of creativity is that it can lead to new and innovative solutions to problems. When faced with a challenge, someone who is creative can come up with unique approaches that may not have been considered before. This can be especially valuable in industries such as technology or healthcare, where innovative solutions can save lives or revolutionize the industry.

Another benefit of creativity is that it can lead to greater job satisfaction. When employees are given the opportunity to use their creative abilities, they are often more engaged in their work and feel a greater sense of fulfillment. This can lead to higher productivity, lower turnover rates, and a more positive workplace culture overall.

However, not developing creativity can lead to a number of problems. Without creativity, individuals or businesses may become stagnant, relying on the same old ideas and approaches without ever trying something new. This can lead to missed opportunities, decreased innovation, and ultimately, a decline in success.

To develop creativity, one can start by challenging themselves to think differently and approach problems in new ways. This can involve brainstorming sessions with colleagues, seeking out new experiences or hobbies, or taking risks and trying something new. It's also important to cultivate a mindset that encourages experimentation and doesn't fear failure, as some of the most creative solutions come from trial and error.

**Innovation:**

Innovation refers to the process of creating something new or improving upon existing products, services, or processes. It involves generating and implementing new ideas, methods, or technologies to address a specific problem or to meet a need. Innovation is essential for progress and growth in every sector, including business, technology, healthcare, and education.

Innovation requires creativity, critical thinking, and

problem-solving skills. It involves identifying areas for improvement or opportunities for change, developing new ideas or concepts, and testing and implementing them. Innovators are constantly seeking new ways to do things better, faster, and more efficiently.

Innovation is also closely linked with entrepreneurship, as many successful businesses are built on innovative ideas and products. Successful entrepreneurs are often those who are able to identify gaps in the market and create new products or services to fill them.

Overall, innovation plays a vital role in driving progress and growth in all aspects of life, and developing innovative thinking skills can help individuals and organizations stay ahead of the curve and thrive in a constantly evolving world.

Alignment of creativity and innovation is essential for success in today's fast-paced and ever-changing business world. A company that is able to foster a culture of creativity and innovation is better equipped to adapt to changing market conditions and stay ahead of the competition.

To align creativity and innovation, companies need to create an environment that encourages and supports creative thinking. This can be achieved through various initiatives such as providing training and development programs that teach employees how to generate new ideas, encouraging cross-functional collaboration, and allowing employees the freedom to experiment and take risks.

Companies also need to establish processes and systems that support the innovation process, such as dedicated research and development teams, idea incubators, and structured innovation processes.

Finally, it's important to have a leadership team that is committed to promoting and supporting creativity and innovation throughout the organization. This includes recognizing and rewarding employees for their contributions, creating a culture of open communication and feedback, and fostering a mindset of continuous improvement.

In conclusion, aligning creativity and innovation is essential for companies looking to stay competitive and thrive in today's business world. By fostering a culture of creativity and innovation, establishing processes and systems to support the innovation process, and having a committed leadership team, companies can achieve sustained success and drive long-term growth.

# Hardwork

Hard work is a crucial element of success in any aspect of life, whether it be personal, professional, or academic. It is the effort and dedication put into achieving a goal or completing a task that sets apart those who succeed from those who do not.

Hard work requires perseverance, discipline, and consistency. It involves setting specific goals and putting in the time and effort needed to achieve them. It requires going above and beyond what is expected and putting in the extra effort needed to succeed.

One of the key benefits of hard work is that it builds character and develops a strong work ethic. It teaches individuals to take responsibility for their actions and to work towards their goals with determination and focus.

However, it is important to note that hard work alone does not guarantee success. It must be coupled with the right attitude, skills, and opportunities to truly achieve one's goals. Additionally, it is important to find a balance between hard work and self-care, as overworking oneself can lead to burnout and other negative consequences.

In conclusion, hard work is a vital component of success in any area of life. It requires dedication, perseverance, and consistency, and helps to build character and develop a strong work ethic. While it is not a guarantee for success, it is a necessary step towards achieving one's goals and aspirations.

While it is possible to achieve some things without hard work, it is unlikely that one can achieve significant success or accomplish their long-term goals without it. In general, hard work is necessary to achieve anything that is worthwhile and meaningful.

Without hard work, individuals may rely on luck or external circumstances to achieve their goals, which can be unreliable and unpredictable. Hard work, on the other hand, is something that individuals have control over, and it allows them to take an active role in shaping their own future.

Furthermore, hard work is often necessary to develop the skills, knowledge, and experience needed to succeed in any given field. It takes time and effort to become proficient in a particular area, and hard work is often required to acquire the necessary expertise.

In conclusion, while it is possible to achieve some things without hard work, significant success and long-term goals typically require a strong work ethic and a dedication to putting in the necessary effort. Hard work is often the key ingredient to achieving one's aspirations and making a meaningful impact in one's life and the lives of others.

One can gain many benefits and rewards with hard work, both personally and professionally. Some examples are:

Achieving goals: One of the most significant benefits of hard work is the ability to achieve one's goals. Hard work allows individuals to make progress towards their objectives, and to accomplish things that they may have thought were impossible.

Increased self-confidence: When individuals put in the effort and dedication needed to succeed, they often experience a boost in self-confidence. They gain a sense of pride and accomplishment that comes from knowing that they have achieved something through their own hard work.

Improved skills and knowledge: Hard work often involves learning new skills, acquiring knowledge, and gaining experience. By putting in the time and effort to improve their abilities, individuals can become more proficient and knowledgeable in their field.

Better opportunities: Hard work can open up new opportunities and lead to career advancement. Employers often recognize and reward hard work, and may offer promotions, bonuses, or other opportunities for growth.

Enhanced reputation: Individuals who are known for their hard work and dedication often have a strong reputation and are respected by their peers and colleagues. This can lead to greater influence and opportunities for collaboration and leadership.

Hard work can lead to a range of benefits and rewards, both tangible and intangible. It requires effort and dedication, but the results can be well worth the investment.

# Strong Interpersonal Skills

Strong interpersonal skills play a vital role in personal and professional success. Interpersonal skills refer to the ability to communicate effectively with others, build relationships, and work well in a team environment.

Here is how strong interpersonal skills can benefit individuals:

Building relationships: Strong interpersonal skills help individuals build positive relationships with others. This is important in both personal and professional contexts, as it can lead to new opportunities, friendships, and collaborations.

Effective communication: Interpersonal skills help individuals communicate effectively with others. This involves not only being able to express oneself clearly but also being able to listen actively and understand others' perspectives.

Conflict resolution: Strong interpersonal skills can help individuals navigate and resolve conflicts. When conflicts arise, individuals with strong interpersonal skills can work towards finding a mutually beneficial solution and maintaining positive relationships.

Leadership: Interpersonal skills are essential for effective leadership. Leaders with strong interpersonal skills can inspire and motivate others, build strong teams, and communicate effectively with stakeholders.

Career success: Interpersonal skills are often considered just as important as technical skills in the workplace. Individuals with strong interpersonal skills are often more successful in their careers, as they can build positive relationships with colleagues, communicate effectively, and navigate complex social dynamics.

Overall, strong interpersonal skills are essential for success in many areas of life. They can help individuals build positive relationships, communicate effectively, and navigate social dynamics, which are all important for personal and professional success.

If one does not develop strong interpersonal skills, it can have negative consequences in both personal and professional settings. Some examples are:

Difficulty building relationships: Individuals who lack strong interpersonal skills may struggle to build positive relationships with others. This can make it challenging to make friends, form romantic relationships, and network professionally.

Misunderstandings and miscommunications: Poor interpersonal skills can lead to misunderstandings and miscommunications with others. This can cause conflicts, lead to mistakes, and damage relationships.

Inability to navigate social dynamics: In both personal and professional settings, social dynamics can be complex. Individuals who lack strong interpersonal skills may struggle to navigate these dynamics effectively, leading to isolation, exclusion, or other negative consequences.

Difficulty with teamwork: Teamwork is an essential part of many jobs and projects. Individuals with poor interpersonal skills may struggle to work well in a team environment, leading to reduced productivity and effectiveness.

Limitations in career advancement: Interpersonal skills are often considered essential for career advancement. Individuals who lack strong interpersonal skills may struggle to network, communicate effectively with colleagues and supervisors, and build positive relationships, limiting their career prospects.

Overall, developing strong interpersonal skills is essential for success in many areas of life. It requires effort and practice, but the benefits are well worth the investment. By improving interpersonal skills, individuals can build positive relationships, communicate effectively, navigate social dynamics, work well in a team environment, and advance in their careers.

# Emotional Intelligence

Emotional intelligence (EI) refers to the ability to recognize, understand, and manage one's own emotions, as well as the emotions of others. It involves a range of skills and abilities, including self-awareness, self-regulation, motivation, empathy, and social skills.

Individuals with high emotional intelligence are often able to navigate social situations effectively, build positive relationships, and manage their own emotions in a healthy and productive way. They are also often able to recognize and respond appropriately to the emotions of others, which can help them build stronger relationships and communicate more effectively.

There are several models of emotional intelligence, but one of the most widely recognized is the model developed by psychologist Daniel Goleman. According to Goleman, emotional intelligence consists of five key components: self-awareness, self-regulation, motivation, empathy, and social skills.

Self-awareness involves being able to recognize and understand one's own emotions, as well as the impact that those emotions have on one's thoughts and behavior. Self-regulation involves the ability to manage one's own emotions effectively, particularly in situations that are challenging or stressful. Motivation involves being able to harness one's emotions in a way that is productive and focused towards achieving goals. Empathy involves being able to recognize and understand the emotions of others, and to respond appropriately to those emotions. Social skills involve the ability to navigate social situations effectively, build positive relationships, and communicate effectively with others.

Emotional intelligence can help individuals build positive relationships, communicate effectively, and navigate social situations in a healthy and productive way.

Emotional intelligence (EI) is increasingly recognized as a critical factor in personal and professional success. Here are some reasons why emotional intelligence is important:

Improved relationships: Individuals with high EI are often able to build strong, positive relationships with others. They are able to recognize and respond appropriately to the emotions of others, which can help them build trust and foster deeper connections.

Effective communication: Effective communication requires both self-awareness and empathy. Individuals with high EI are often able to communicate more effectively, both in terms of expressing their own emotions and understanding the emotions of others.

Conflict resolution: Conflict is a natural part of relationships, but learning to manage conflicts effectively can help to strengthen those relationships. Individuals with high EI are often able to manage conflicts in a way that is productive and focused on finding mutually beneficial solutions.

Leadership: Leaders with high EI are often more effective in managing and motivating teams. They are able to recognize and respond to the emotions of team members, build trust, and create a positive work environment.

Personal growth: Developing emotional intelligence requires self-reflection and self-awareness, which can lead to personal growth and development. Individuals with high EI are often able to manage their own emotions effectively, stay motivated, and achieve their goals.

Overall, emotional intelligence is an important factor in personal and professional success. By developing emotional intelligence, individuals can build stronger relationships, communicate effectively, manage conflicts, lead effectively, and achieve their goals.

# Risk Taking

Risk refers to the potential for harm or loss as a result of taking an action or making a decision. It involves uncertainty and the possibility of negative consequences. The level of risk involved in any situation depends on the likelihood of a negative outcome and the potential impact of that outcome.

In everyday life, we encounter different types of risks, such as financial risk, health risk, career risk, and social risk. For example, investing in the stock market carries financial risk because there is a chance of losing money, while not wearing a helmet while riding a bike carries health risk because it increases the chances of injury in case of an accident.

In general, the concept of risk is important to understand because it can help us make informed decisions by evaluating the potential rewards and consequences of our actions.

Risk-taking is the act of making decisions or taking actions that involve uncertainty, and may result in either positive or negative outcomes. Here are some key points to consider when it comes to risk-taking:

Risk-taking is necessary for growth: Taking risks is essential for personal and professional growth. Without taking risks, it is difficult to learn and develop new skills, expand your comfort zone, or achieve your goals.

Identify and evaluate risks: Before taking any risks, it is important to identify and evaluate the potential risks and benefits. Consider the potential consequences of your actions, and weigh the risks against the potential rewards.

Take calculated risks: While taking risks is important, it is also important to take calculated risks. This means taking risks that are well thought-out, and based on a thorough evaluation of the potential risks and rewards.

Learn from failure: Failure is a natural part of taking risks. Rather than seeing failure as a negative outcome, view it as an opportunity to learn and grow. Analyze your failures, identify what went wrong, and use that information to inform your future decisions.

Develop resilience: Taking risks can be challenging, and it is important to develop resilience in order to cope with the potential setbacks and failures that may occur. Resilience involves developing a positive mindset, focusing on solutions rather than problems, and developing coping strategies to help you manage stress and adversity.

Overall, taking risks is an essential part of personal and professional growth. By identifying and evaluating risks, taking calculated risks, learning from failure, developing resilience, and continuously learning and growing, you can become more comfortable with risk-taking and achieve your goals.

Risk-taking can be both good and bad, depending on the situation and the risks involved. Here are some factors to consider when evaluating the potential risks and benefits of taking a risk:

Potential rewards: Taking risks can lead to positive outcomes, such as personal or professional growth, financial gain, or achievement of a goal.

Potential consequences: Risks can also have negative consequences, such as financial loss, physical harm, or damage to personal or professional relationships.

Probability of success: Consider the likelihood of success and failure when evaluating a risk. If the probability of success is high and the potential rewards outweigh the potential consequences, it may be worth taking the risk.

Your tolerance for risk: Everyone has a different tolerance for risk. Some people are more comfortable with uncertainty and are willing to take bigger risks, while others are more risk-averse and prefer to take more cautious approaches.

Context and timing: The context and timing of a risk can also affect whether it is a good or bad decision. For example, taking a risk in a supportive environment with the right resources and support may be more likely to lead to success than taking the same risk in a high-pressure, unsupportive environment.

Overall, taking risks can be both good and bad. It is important to carefully evaluate the potential risks and rewards, consider your own tolerance for risk, and make decisions based on the specific context and timing of the situation.

Taking a calculated risk means carefully evaluating the potential rewards and consequences of a decision before making a move. Here are some steps you can take to take a calculated risk:

Define your goal: Clearly define the goal that you want to achieve. This will help you to determine if the potential risk is worth taking.

Gather information: Collect as much information as possible about the risk, including the likelihood of success, potential costs, and potential benefits.

Analyze the data: Analyze the information that you have gathered to determine the potential risks and benefits of taking the risk.

Develop a plan: Develop a plan for how you will take the risk, including contingency plans for dealing with potential negative outcomes.

Consider the consequences: Consider the potential consequences of the risk, both positive and negative, and decide if the potential benefits outweigh the potential risks.

Take action: Once you have evaluated the risk and developed a plan, take action and execute your plan.

Evaluate the results: After taking the risk, evaluate the results and learn from your experience. This will help you to make better decisions in the future.

# Confidence

Confidence is the belief in oneself, one's abilities, qualities, and judgment. It is a crucial trait for personal and professional growth, as it allows individuals to take risks, overcome obstacles, and achieve success. Confidence is essential in all aspects of life, including work, relationships, and personal endeavors.

Having confidence leads to several benefits. Some of them are:

Improved performance: When an individual believes in their abilities, they are more likely to perform well in their tasks.

Better communication skills: Confidence allows individuals to express themselves effectively and assertively.

Positive self-image: Confidence leads to a positive self-image, which can improve mental health and well-being.

Resilience: Confident individuals are better equipped to handle setbacks and challenges, as they believe in their ability to overcome obstacles.

Increased opportunities: Confidence can lead to increased opportunities in career, relationships, and personal growth.

Confidence is an essential trait for personal and professional success, and developing confidence can lead to numerous benefits.

Confidence is particularly important during tough times because it can help you stay focused and motivated even when faced with challenges and obstacles. Here are some ways in which confidence can be helpful during tough times:

Confidence can help you stay calm: When you are confident, you are better able to handle stressful situations without becoming overwhelmed. You can approach difficult situations with a sense of calmness and clarity, which can help you make better decisions.

Confidence can help you stay focused: During tough times, it can be easy to get distracted or lose sight of your goals. But when you have confidence in yourself and your abilities, you can stay focused on what you need to do to overcome the challenges you face.

Confidence can help you stay motivated: When things get tough, it can be tempting to give up or lose motivation. But when you have confidence in yourself and your ability to succeed, you are more likely to stay motivated and keep working towards your goals.

Confidence can help you bounce back: Tough times can be discouraging, but when you have confidence in yourself, you are better able to bounce back from setbacks and keep moving forward.

# Time Management

Time management is the process of planning, organizing, and prioritizing how much time you spend on different activities to maximize productivity and achieve your goals. It involves setting clear goals, identifying important tasks, creating a schedule, and allocating time for each task. Effective time management allows you to make the most of the time you have, avoid procrastination, reduce stress, and achieve your goals in a timely manner. By managing your time well, you can increase your productivity, improve your work-life balance, and create more time for the things you enjoy.

Time is valuable because it is a finite resource. Once time is gone, it can never be regained. Unlike money or other resources, time is limited and cannot be replenished. Every moment we have is precious, and how we use our time determines our quality of life. Time is the one resource that is truly universal, as everyone has the same amount of time in a day, and how we choose to use it can make all the difference. By managing our time effectively and using it wisely, we can achieve our goals, fulfill our potential, and live a meaningful and fulfilling life.

Effective time management is important for several reasons:

Increased productivity: By managing your time effectively, you can accomplish more in less time. This allows you to be more productive and achieve your goals more efficiently.

Reduced stress: Poor time management can lead to stress and anxiety as tasks pile up and deadlines approach. By managing your time effectively, you can reduce stress and avoid last-minute rushes.

Improved quality of work: Effective time management allows you to allocate sufficient time to each task, which can improve the quality of your work. By avoiding rushed or incomplete work, you can produce better results and achieve greater success.

Better work-life balance: Effective time management can help you to balance your work and personal life. By scheduling your time carefully, you can make time for the things that matter most, such as family, friends, and hobbies.

Increased motivation: By accomplishing tasks efficiently and effectively, you can feel a sense of achievement and satisfaction. This can increase your motivation and help you to stay focused and productive.

# Leadership

Leadership is the ability to inspire and guide others towards a common goal or vision. Effective leadership involves setting clear goals, communicating effectively, making decisions, inspiring and motivating others, and taking responsibility for the outcomes of the team.

Leadership can be displayed in various settings, such as in the workplace, in community organizations, in politics, and in personal relationships. A good leader is someone who is able to build trust and establish strong relationships with their followers, while also providing direction and guidance.

Leadership is an important skill to develop because it can have a significant impact on the success of an organization or a team. Effective leaders can create a positive work environment, increase motivation and productivity, and inspire innovation and creativity.

There are many different approaches to leadership, including transformational leadership, servant leadership, and situational leadership. Each approach has its own strengths and weaknesses, and different styles may be more effective in different situations.

Ultimately, effective leadership requires a combination of skills, including communication, decision-making, problem-solving, and emotional intelligence. By developing these skills, individuals can become effective leaders who are able to inspire and guide others towards a common goal or vision.

If a group or organization does not have effective leadership, it can have negative consequences. Without leadership, there may be confusion about the direction of the group or organization, leading to a lack of focus and coordination. This can result in missed opportunities, inefficiencies, and lower productivity.

In the absence of leadership, there may also be a lack of accountability and responsibility. Without someone to take charge and make decisions, it can be difficult to assign responsibility for the outcomes of the group or organization.

Moreover, without effective leadership, there may be a lack of motivation and engagement among the members of the group or organization. A good leader is able to inspire and motivate others towards a common goal or vision, while also providing direction and guidance. Without this guidance and motivation, members may become disengaged and less productive.

However, leadership can come from anyone, regardless of their title or position. In the absence of formal leadership, individuals can step up and take on leadership roles, providing guidance and direction for the group or organization. By developing leadership skills, individuals can help to fill this gap and ensure the success of the group or organization.

Just like Leadership, Teamwork is also an important element. It is essential in most aspects of life, whether it's in the workplace, in sports, or in personal relationships.

Here are some reasons why teamwork is important:

Increased productivity: When people work together, they can share ideas, knowledge, and skills, which can lead to more efficient and effective solutions. This can result in increased productivity and better outcomes.

Better communication: Teamwork promotes open communication, which can help to avoid misunderstandings and conflicts. This can lead to better relationships among team members and a more positive work environment.

Increased creativity: When people work together, they can brainstorm and come up with new and innovative ideas that they might not have thought of on their own.

Shared responsibility: Teamwork allows for the workload to be shared among team members, which can reduce stress and prevent burnout. It also promotes a sense of shared responsibility for the success of the team.

Improved problem-solving: When people work together, they can tackle complex problems that might be difficult to solve on their own. This can lead to more creative and effective solutions.

Overall, teamwork is important because it promotes collaboration, communication, creativity, shared responsibility, and problem-solving. These are all important skills and qualities that are valued in most areas of life, whether it's in the workplace, in sports, or in personal relationships.

# Humility

Humility is a quality or characteristic of being modest, respectful, and humble. It involves having a sense of modesty about one's own achievements, skills, and abilities, and a willingness to acknowledge and learn from one's limitations and mistakes. A person who possesses humility is often seen as approachable, empathetic, and open-minded, and is respected for their willingness to listen to and learn from others.

Humility can be seen as a fundamental trait of emotional intelligence, as it involves recognizing and managing one's own emotions and being aware of how one's behavior impacts others. It is also a trait valued in many cultures and religions as a way to cultivate a sense of respect and reverence for others, as well as for oneself.

Humility is an important quality that can help individuals to build stronger relationships, promote learning and growth, and become effective leaders. It involves recognizing and accepting one's limitations while striving to be the best version of oneself.

Humility is the quality of being modest, respectful, and humble. It involves recognizing and accepting one's limitations and mistakes, as well as acknowledging the strengths and achievements of others.

Here are some reasons why humility is important:

Builds stronger relationships: When you are humble, you are more approachable, relatable, and open to feedback. This can help to build stronger relationships with others and create a more positive and supportive environment.

Promotes learning and growth: Humility involves acknowledging your limitations and mistakes, which can help you to identify areas for improvement and take steps towards growth and development.

Enhances leadership: Humility is an important quality for effective leadership, as it helps leaders to build trust and respect among their team members. Humble leaders are more likely to listen to their team members, acknowledge their contributions, and make decisions that benefit the team as a whole.

Reduces conflict: When you are humble, you are less likely to be defensive or confrontational, which can help to reduce conflicts and promote a more collaborative and harmonious environment.

Fosters gratitude: Humility involves recognizing and appreciating the contributions of others, which can help to foster gratitude and a sense of interconnectedness.

Overall, humility is an important quality that can help to build stronger relationships, promote learning and growth, enhance leadership, reduce conflict, and foster gratitude.

If one lacks humility, they may struggle with building strong relationships with others, learning and growing, and being an effective leader. They may come across as arrogant or defensive, which can create a negative and unapproachable persona. They may also have difficulty acknowledging their mistakes and taking responsibility for their actions, which can lead to a lack of accountability and trust among their peers.

Without humility, it can be challenging to develop the self-awareness and emotional intelligence needed to navigate complex social situations, handle conflicts, and build positive relationships. Additionally, it can be difficult to learn from others and grow in areas where one may be lacking.

However, it is never too late to develop humility. One can work on cultivating this quality by practicing active listening, acknowledging and learning from mistakes, being open to feedback, and recognizing the strengths and achievements of others. With practice and intention, humility can be developed and become an integral part of one's personality and behavior.

# Self Awareness

Self-awareness is the ability to recognize and understand one's own emotions, thoughts, and behaviors. It involves being aware of one's strengths and weaknesses, and having a clear understanding of how one's actions impact others. Self-awareness allows individuals to gain insights into their own motivations, needs, and values, which can be used to make better decisions, improve relationships, and achieve personal growth.

Self-awareness is important for several reasons:

Personal growth: By understanding your own thoughts, emotions, and behaviors, you can identify areas for improvement and take steps towards personal growth.

Effective communication: Self-awareness helps you to better understand your own communication style and how it may be perceived by others. This allows you to adjust your communication to be more effective in different situations.

Better decision-making: Self-awareness helps you to make more informed decisions by considering your own values, beliefs, and goals.

Improved relationships: When you are aware of your own emotions and behaviors, you can better understand the emotions and behaviors of others, which can improve your relationships.

Increased resilience: Self-awareness allows you to identify and manage your own emotions, which can help you to better cope with stress and adversity.

Overall, self-awareness is important for personal and professional growth, effective communication, and building strong relationships with others.

If an individual lacks self-awareness, they may struggle with personal growth, effective communication, and building strong relationships with others. They may also have difficulty making informed decisions, as they may not be fully aware of their own values, beliefs, and goals.
Lack of self-awareness can also lead to misunderstandings and conflicts with others, as individuals may not be fully aware of how their actions and behaviors are perceived by others. They may also struggle with managing their emotions, which can lead to stress and difficulty coping with adversity.
However, the good news is that self-awareness can be developed and improved through various practices and techniques, such as self-reflection, mindfulness, and seeking feedback from others. By developing self-awareness, individuals can become more in-tune with their own emotions, thoughts, and behaviors, and make positive changes in their personal and professional lives.

# Curiosity

Curiosity is the natural human desire to explore, learn, and understand new things. It is the urge to ask questions, seek answers, and engage with the world around us. Curiosity can drive us to seek new experiences, challenge our assumptions, and push the boundaries of what we know and understand. It is an essential trait for personal growth, intellectual development, and innovation.

Curiosity can have many benefits in our personal and professional lives. Here are a few examples:

Learning: Curiosity drives us to seek out new knowledge and information. It helps us learn and understand new concepts, which can lead to personal and professional growth.

Creativity: Curiosity can spark creativity and innovation. By asking questions and exploring new ideas, we can generate new solutions and approaches to problems.

Empathy: Curiosity can help us develop empathy and understanding for others. By asking questions and trying to see things from different perspectives, we can develop more meaningful relationships and better communication skills.

Resilience: Curiosity can help us develop resilience and a growth mindset. By embracing challenges and seeking out new experiences, we can develop the skills and mindset needed to overcome obstacles and adapt to change.

Enjoyment: Curiosity can simply make life more enjoyable. It can lead us to new experiences and adventures, which can bring a sense of fulfillment and happiness.

Overall, curiosity is a powerful tool for personal and professional development, and can help us lead more fulfilling and satisfying lives.

While curiosity is generally seen as a positive trait, excessive curiosity can have some adverse effects.

Distraction: Excessive curiosity can lead to distraction from important tasks and responsibilities.

Intrusiveness: If curiosity is not managed properly, it can lead to intrusiveness and invading other people's privacy.

Risk-taking behavior: Curiosity can lead to risk-taking behavior, especially if the curiosity involves dangerous or prohibited activities.

Information overload: Too much curiosity can result in information overload, which can lead to confusion and overwhelm.

Anxiety: Excessive curiosity can lead to anxiety and stress, especially if the curiosity is focused on negative or worrying subjects.

It is important to find a balance between curiosity and other important aspects of life, such as work, relationships, and personal health.

# Communication

Communication is the process of exchanging information or ideas between individuals or groups. It involves sending and receiving messages through verbal or nonverbal means, such as speaking, writing, body language, and facial expressions. Communication can occur in various forms, including interpersonal, organizational, and mass communication. Effective communication is essential for building relationships, sharing information, expressing thoughts and feelings, and achieving goals. It involves not only transmitting information but also active listening, understanding, and responding appropriately to the message received.

Communication skills are incredibly important for success in all aspects of life, including personal relationships, education, career, and leadership. Effective communication allows individuals to express their thoughts and ideas clearly, listen and understand others, build strong relationships, and collaborate effectively with others towards a common goal. In contrast, poor communication skills can lead to misunderstandings, conflicts, and missed opportunities. Therefore, developing strong communication skills is essential for personal and professional growth and success.

Effective communication is crucial to achieving success in various areas of life, including personal, professional, and social.

Here are some ways in which communication can help in the process of success:

Building relationships: Communication helps in building positive relationships with people, including family, friends, colleagues, and clients. Strong relationships based on effective communication can lead to better collaboration, increased trust, and mutual support.

Sharing ideas and knowledge: Effective communication allows individuals to share their ideas, knowledge, and expertise with others. This can lead to the generation of new ideas, better problem-solving, and innovation.

Setting and achieving goals: Communication plays a vital role in setting and achieving goals. Clear communication helps in defining goals, establishing timelines, identifying obstacles, and developing strategies to overcome them.

Resolving conflicts: Communication is essential in resolving conflicts that may arise in personal or professional relationships. Effective communication skills can help in de-escalating conflicts, understanding the perspectives of others, and finding mutually agreeable solutions.

Building a positive reputation: Good communication skills can help in building a positive reputation in personal and professional settings. Effective communication can help in projecting a confident and competent image, establishing credibility, and inspiring trust and respect.

In summary, effective communication is critical for success in various aspects of life. It allows individuals to build relationships, share ideas and knowledge, set and achieve goals, resolve conflicts, and build a positive reputation.

Bad communication can have several adverse effects, including:

Misunderstandings: Poor communication can lead to misunderstandings, confusion, and mistakes. This can result in delays, rework, and even project failure.

Conflict: Miscommunication can lead to conflicts and arguments among team members, which can harm relationships and affect team performance.

Low morale: Poor communication can also lead to low morale among team members. When people don't know what's expected of them or feel ignored, they can become demotivated and disengaged.

Lost opportunities: Ineffective communication can cause missed opportunities, such as failing to win a new client or missing a deadline.

Damage to reputation: Poor communication can also damage the reputation of an individual or organization. Negative word-of-mouth can spread quickly, leading to lost business and opportunities.

Overall, bad communication can have a significant impact on an individual's or organization's success. It is important to develop strong communication skills to avoid these adverse effects.

# Gratitude

Gratitude is the quality of being thankful and showing appreciation for what one has in life, rather than focusing on what one lacks or desires. It involves acknowledging and recognizing the good things in one's life and being mindful of the positive aspects of each day. Practicing gratitude can help to foster a positive attitude and increase feelings of happiness, contentment, and overall well-being. It can also improve relationships and increase social connections, as expressing gratitude towards others can build stronger bonds and foster a sense of community.

Expressing gratitude is important because it has many benefits for both our mental and physical health. When we practice gratitude, it helps us to focus on the positive aspects of our lives and can shift our mindset from one of lack to one of abundance. This can lead to increased feelings of happiness, satisfaction, and overall well-being.

Expressing gratitude can also improve our relationships with others, as it can help us to connect with them on a deeper level and build stronger bonds. It can also foster a sense of empathy and understanding, which can lead to more compassionate and meaningful interactions with others.

In addition to these emotional and social benefits, research has also shown that practicing gratitude can have physical health benefits, such as reducing stress levels, improving sleep quality, and boosting the immune system.

Overall, expressing gratitude is a simple yet powerful way to improve our quality of life and cultivate a more positive outlook on the world around us.

There are several ways to express gratitude, some of them are:

Saying Thank You: The most common way of expressing gratitude is by simply saying thank you. It can be done in person, over the phone, or in writing.

Writing a Gratitude Journal: A gratitude journal is a place where you can write down things you are grateful for. It can be a daily, weekly or monthly practice that helps you focus on the positive things in your life.

Giving a Gift: Giving a gift to someone is a way of expressing gratitude. It could be as simple as a card or as elaborate as a thoughtful present.

Paying it Forward: One way to show gratitude is by helping someone else. When you receive help or kindness, you can pay it forward by helping someone else.

Acts of Service: Doing something kind for someone else is another way to express gratitude. It could be as simple as running an errand or as complex as volunteering your time for a cause.

Giving Compliments: Giving compliments is a way of expressing gratitude for someone's actions or qualities. It can make someone feel appreciated and valued.

Expressing Gratitude in Prayer or Meditation: Many people express gratitude through prayer or meditation. It is a way of acknowledging and thanking a higher power for the blessings in life.

It is important to be grateful for what we do. Being grateful for the work we do can help increase our job satisfaction, motivation, and productivity. It can also help us maintain a positive attitude towards our work and colleagues, even during challenging times. Expressing gratitude for our job can also help us appreciate the opportunities and benefits that come with it, such as a steady income, professional growth, and work-life balance. In turn, this can help us achieve a greater sense of fulfillment and happiness in our careers.

# Knowing Oneself

Knowing oneself refers to the process of understanding one's own thoughts, feelings, behaviors, and characteristics. It involves gaining insights into one's values, strengths, weaknesses, beliefs, motivations, and aspirations. Knowing oneself can help individuals make better decisions, set more meaningful goals, build healthier relationships, and enhance their overall well-being. It involves self-reflection, introspection, and a willingness to examine oneself honestly and without judgment. By knowing oneself, individuals can develop greater self-awareness, self-acceptance, and self-confidence.

Knowing oneself can have several benefits, including:

Self-awareness: Knowing oneself helps to develop a better understanding of one's own emotions, thoughts, and behaviors, which in turn can help in making better decisions and managing emotions effectively.

Personal growth: When you know yourself better, you can identify your strengths and weaknesses and work on personal growth to enhance your strengths and overcome weaknesses.

Improved relationships: Understanding oneself better can help to improve relationships with others by developing better communication skills, empathy, and understanding of others' perspectives.

Increased confidence: Knowing oneself can lead to increased confidence, as you have a better understanding of your own values, beliefs, and goals.

Fulfillment: When you know yourself better, you can align your actions with your values, which can lead to a sense of purpose and fulfillment in life.

Overall, knowing oneself is an essential aspect of personal development and can lead to a more fulfilling and meaningful life.

Knowing oneself is an essential aspect of achieving success. When you know yourself, you are aware of your strengths, weaknesses, values, beliefs, and motivations. This knowledge enables you to set realistic goals that align with your interests and abilities, which increases the likelihood of achieving them. Additionally, knowing yourself helps you to make better decisions and take actions that are in line with your authentic self, leading to greater fulfillment and satisfaction in life.

It also helps you to manage stress and overcome obstacles more effectively by understanding how you react to certain situations and identifying coping mechanisms that work for you. Finally, self-awareness can also improve your interpersonal relationships, as it helps you to understand and empathize with others' perspectives and communicate more effectively with them. All these factors contribute to achieving success in various aspects of life, such as career, relationships, personal growth, and well-being.

# How to achieve them

## **Passion, Purpose, and Ambition:**

Identify your values: Determine what is important to you and what drives you. These values will help guide you in making decisions about your passions, purpose, and ambitions.

Discover your passion: Find out what makes you happy and gives you a sense of fulfillment. Try different activities and hobbies until you find something that excites you.

Set specific goals: Define what you want to achieve in life and set specific goals to work towards. Break down your goals into smaller, achievable steps.

Create a plan: Develop a roadmap to help you achieve your goals. Create an action plan and timeline, and adjust as needed.

Take action: Start taking action towards your goals. Consistently work towards them and hold yourself accountable.

Cultivate a growth mindset: Embrace challenges and mistakes as opportunities to learn and grow. Stay curious and open to new ideas.

Network and build relationships: Build connections with people who share similar interests and can offer support and advice. Seek mentors and role models who inspire you.

Practice self-care: Take care of your physical, emotional, and mental health. Make time for rest, exercise regularly, and practice mindfulness and stress management techniques.

Continuously learn and improve: Seek out opportunities for learning and development. Take courses, read books, attend workshops and conferences, and stay up-to-date with industry trends.

Stay committed and persistent: Stay focused on your goals and maintain your motivation and drive. Celebrate your successes along the way, and learn from any setbacks or failures.

## **Focus and Concentration:**

Identify your goals and prioritize them. When you know what you want to achieve, you can focus your efforts on the most important tasks.

Create a schedule or routine that allows you to dedicate specific times to work on your tasks. This will help you avoid distractions and interruptions.

Set specific and achievable goals for each work session. This will give you a sense of accomplishment and keep you motivated.

Eliminate or minimize distractions, such as social media, phone notifications, or unnecessary noise.

Take breaks to recharge your energy and refresh your mind. Short, frequent breaks are more effective than longer, infrequent ones.

Practice mindfulness or meditation to improve your ability to focus and quiet your mind.

Exercise regularly to improve your physical and mental health, which can help improve your focus and concentration.

Get enough sleep and maintain a healthy diet. A well-rested and nourished body and brain are better able to concentrate and focus.

Create a positive and inspiring work environment that stimulates your creativity and motivation.

Continuously evaluate and adjust your strategies to achieve optimal results. Be open to feedback and willing to try new approaches.

## **Continuous Learning:**

Identify your learning goals: Identify what you want to learn and why it is important to you. Create a list of topics that you want to learn more about.

Develop a learning plan: Once you have identified your learning goals, create a learning plan that outlines the steps you need to take to achieve those goals. Break the plan down into smaller, manageable tasks.

Make time for learning: Schedule dedicated time for learning each day or week. Create a routine that you can stick to.

Choose your learning resources: Select resources that align with your learning goals. This could include books, online courses, webinars, podcasts, or other materials.

Engage with others: Engage with others who share similar learning goals or interests. Join a community, attend conferences or seminars, or find a mentor.

Stay organized: Keep track of your learning progress and organize your notes, resources, and materials in a way that is easy to access.

Practice active learning: Actively engage with the material you are learning by taking notes, asking questions, and summarizing key concepts.

Apply what you learn: Apply what you learn to real-world situations. Practice using new skills and knowledge in your daily life.

Reflect on your learning: Reflect on what you have learned and how you can apply it in the future. Consider what worked well and what you could do differently next time.

Continuously update your learning plan: Continuously update your learning plan as you achieve your goals and discover new areas you want to learn about. Regularly review your progress and adjust your plan as needed.

## Positive Attitude:

Identify negative thoughts: The first step to developing a positive attitude is to identify negative thoughts that you might be having. Negative thoughts can limit your potential and prevent you from achieving your goals.

Replace negative thoughts with positive ones: Once you have identified your negative thoughts, replace them with positive ones. For example, instead of thinking "I can't do this," replace it with "I can do this if I put my mind to it."

Practice gratitude: Take time to appreciate the good things in your life, no matter how small they may seem. Gratitude helps shift your focus from what you don't have to what you do have.

Surround yourself with positive people: The people you spend time with can have a big impact on your attitude. Surround yourself with positive, supportive people who encourage and motivate you.

Practice positive self-talk: The way you talk to yourself can have a big impact on your attitude. Practice positive self-talk by using encouraging phrases such as "I am capable" or "I can do this."

Set realistic goals: Setting goals that are achievable and realistic can help boost your confidence and sense of accomplishment.

Learn from your failures: Instead of dwelling on your failures, use them as an opportunity to learn and grow. Focus on what you can do differently next time to achieve success.

Take care of your physical health: Your physical health can have a big impact on your attitude. Take care of your body by eating healthy, exercising regularly, and getting enough sleep.

Engage in activities you enjoy: Engaging in activities you enjoy can help improve your mood and overall attitude. Make time for hobbies and activities that bring you joy.

Focus on the present moment: Don't let worries about the past or future consume your thoughts. Focus on the present moment and what you can do to make the most of it.

## **Resilience:**

Accept reality: Accepting the situation as it is, instead of denying or resisting it, can help you move forward and focus on what can be done next.

Cultivate optimism: Focus on positive thoughts and outcomes, and try to find opportunities within challenges.

Practice gratitude: Recognize and appreciate the good things in your life, and express gratitude regularly.

Build a strong support system: Surround yourself with people who uplift and support you, and seek help when needed.

Set realistic goals: Break down big goals into smaller, achievable steps, and celebrate progress along the way.

Take care of your physical health: Get enough sleep, exercise regularly, and eat a balanced diet to support your mental and emotional resilience.

Practice mindfulness: Practice being present and aware of your thoughts and emotions, without judgment or attachment.

Learn from setbacks: Instead of dwelling on failures or mistakes, focus on what you can learn from them and how you can improve in the future.

Keep a positive perspective: Look for opportunities in challenges and setbacks, and try to maintain a positive outlook.

Practice self-compassion: Treat yourself with kindness, understanding, and forgiveness, especially during difficult times.

## **<u>Adaptability:</u>**

Recognize the need for adaptability: Start by understanding the importance of adaptability in today's fast-changing world. Realize that being adaptable is a valuable skill that will help you navigate uncertain situations with ease.

Embrace change: Accept that change is inevitable and try to embrace it rather than resist it. Instead of fearing change, see it as an opportunity for growth and learning.

Stay informed: Keep yourself informed about the latest trends and developments in your field of work. Attend conferences, workshops, and seminars to stay updated with the latest industry insights.

Cultivate a growth mindset: Adopt a growth mindset that allows you to learn from your mistakes and failures. See every challenge as an opportunity to learn and grow, rather than a setback.

Practice flexibility: Be open to new ideas and approaches. Be willing to adjust your plans and strategies based on changing circumstances.

Build a strong network: Surround yourself with people who are adaptable and can provide support and guidance when you face challenging situations. Build a network of mentors, colleagues, and friends who can help you navigate difficult times.

Take calculated risks: Be willing to take calculated risks and step out of your comfort zone. This will help you develop the courage and confidence to adapt to new situations.

Learn new skills: Continuously learn new skills that will help you adapt to changing circumstances. This could include learning a new language, developing your communication skills, or improving your technological proficiency.

Practice mindfulness: Practice mindfulness techniques such as meditation and deep breathing to help you stay calm and focused during stressful situations.

Celebrate successes: Celebrate your successes, no matter how small. This will help you stay motivated and build resilience in the face of adversity.

## **Perseverance:**

Define your goal: Be clear about what you want to achieve and why it is important to you. This clarity will help you stay motivated when faced with challenges.

Break down your goal into smaller steps: Dividing your goal into smaller, more manageable steps can help you avoid feeling overwhelmed and can give you a sense of progress.

Create a plan: Once you have broken down your goal into smaller steps, create a plan for how you will achieve each step.

Prioritize: Determine which steps are most important and focus on completing those first.

Stay organized: Use tools such as calendars, to-do lists, and project management software to keep track of your progress and stay on track.

Stay positive: Adopt a positive mindset and focus on the progress you are making, rather than dwelling on setbacks or mistakes.

Learn from failures: View failures as learning opportunities and use them to adjust your approach and improve your chances of success.

Celebrate your successes: Take time to celebrate your accomplishments along the way, even the small ones. This can help you stay motivated and maintain momentum.

Surround yourself with support: Seek out people who can provide encouragement, advice, and accountability to help you stay on track.

Keep going: Finally, remember that perseverance is about staying committed to your goal, even when things get tough. Keep pushing forward and never give up on what you want to achieve.

## **<u>Creativity and Innovation:</u>**

Open your mind: Start by being open to new ideas and experiences. Be willing to explore different perspectives, question assumptions, and challenge the status quo.

Develop a growth mindset: Adopt a mindset that embraces learning and growth. Recognize that failure is an opportunity to learn and that with practice, you can develop new skills and abilities.

Practice curiosity: Cultivate curiosity by asking questions, seeking out new experiences, and actively pursuing knowledge and understanding.

Take risks: Don't be afraid to take risks and try new things. Creativity and innovation often require taking risks and stepping out of your comfort zone.

Practice mindfulness: Practice mindfulness to help quiet your mind and focus your attention. This can help you become more aware of your thoughts and emotions, which can lead to new insights and ideas.

Collaborate with others: Seek out opportunities to collaborate with others. Working with people from different backgrounds and perspectives can lead to new ideas and approaches.

Keep an open mind: Be open to feedback and be willing to revise your ideas and approaches. Sometimes the best ideas come from unexpected sources.

Embrace failure: Recognize that failure is an inevitable part of the creative process. Embrace failure as a learning opportunity and use it to fuel your creativity and innovation.

Practice divergent thinking: Practice divergent thinking, which involves generating multiple ideas and solutions to a problem. This can help you break out of your usual ways of thinking and come up with new and innovative ideas.

Practice creativity regularly: Finally, practice creativity regularly. Just like any other skill, creativity, and innovation require practice and regular exercise. Set aside time each day or week to engage in creative activities, such as brainstorming, sketching, or writing.

## Hardwork:

Set clear goals: Identify what you want to achieve and set clear, specific, and measurable goals. This will help you stay focused and motivated.

Create a plan: Once you have identified your goals, create a plan that outlines the steps you need to take to achieve them. Break your goals down into smaller, more manageable tasks.

Prioritize: Determine which tasks are most important and prioritize them accordingly. This will help you focus on what really matters and avoid wasting time on less important tasks.

Set deadlines: Set realistic deadlines for each task and hold yourself accountable for meeting them.

Stay organized: Keep your workspace clean and organized. This will help you stay focused and minimize distractions.

Eliminate distractions: Identify and eliminate any distractions that may hinder your productivity. This could include social media, email, or other non-work-related tasks.

Take breaks: Take regular breaks throughout the day to rest and recharge. This will help you avoid burnout and maintain your energy levels.

Stay motivated: Find ways to stay motivated, such as tracking your progress, rewarding yourself for achieving milestones, or visualizing your success.

Learn from failure: Embrace failure as a learning opportunity and use it to improve your skills and processes.

Stay committed: Stay committed to your goals and persevere through challenges and setbacks. Remember that hard work and persistence are key to achieving success.

## **<u>Strong Interpersonal Skills:</u>**

Improve your communication skills: Communication is an important part of interpersonal skills. Practice active listening, effective speaking, and clarity in your communication.

Practice empathy: Try to put yourself in other people's shoes to understand their point of view. It will help you build better relationships with them.

Learn to manage conflicts: Conflicts are inevitable in interpersonal relationships. Learn to manage them by developing conflict resolution skills.

Develop emotional intelligence: Emotional intelligence is the ability to recognize and manage your own emotions and those of others. It helps in building better relationships.

Improve your body language: Body language plays an important role in communication. Pay attention to your posture, facial expressions, and gestures.

Build trust: Trust is the foundation of any interpersonal relationship. Be honest, reliable and keep your promises to build trust.

Be respectful: Treat everyone with respect and dignity. Avoid making derogatory comments or using offensive language.

Be a good listener: Listening is an important part of communication. Listen actively to understand the other person's point of view.

Collaborate: Interpersonal skills involve working with others. Learn to collaborate and work in teams to achieve common goals.

Practice self-reflection: Reflect on your own behavior and actions. Identify areas where you need to improve and work on them.

## **<u>Emotional Intelligence:</u>**

Identify your emotions: Start by identifying your emotions as they arise. This will help you become more aware of your emotional state and how it influences your thoughts and behavior.

Practice self-awareness: Take the time to reflect on your own emotional responses to situations. This will help you understand your own emotions and how they impact your interactions with others.

Practice empathy: Try to see things from other people's perspectives and understand how they are feeling. This will help you build stronger relationships and communicate more effectively.

Practice active listening: Listen to what others are saying without judgment and without interrupting. This will help you understand their emotions and respond appropriately.

Develop your communication skills: Learn how to communicate your emotions and thoughts effectively to others. This includes being assertive, but also being sensitive to the emotions of others.

Manage stress effectively: Learn how to manage stress and anxiety so that you can respond to situations calmly and rationally.

Develop positive relationships: Build strong, positive relationships with others by being supportive and understanding.

Practice self-regulation: Learn how to regulate your own emotions so that you can respond appropriately to situations.

Practice problem-solving skills: Develop your problem-solving skills so that you can find solutions to challenges that arise.

Practice self-motivation: Stay motivated and focused on your goals, even in the face of challenges and setbacks. This will help you maintain a positive attitude and outlook.

## **Risk Taking:**

Identify your fears: Start by recognizing what you are afraid of, and what is holding you back from taking risks.

Set realistic goals: Develop a plan of action for your goals, and make sure they are achievable.

Embrace failure: Learn to see failure as an opportunity to learn and grow, rather than something to be avoided at all costs.

Take calculated risks: Weigh the potential benefits against the potential risks of any decision you make.

Trust your instincts: Listen to your gut feelings and trust your intuition.

Seek out new experiences: Step outside of your comfort zone and try new things.

Surround yourself with supportive people: Build a network of people who encourage and motivate you to take risks.

Practice mindfulness: Focus on the present moment and avoid getting distracted by worries or anxieties about the future.

Learn from your mistakes: Take time to reflect on your experiences and learn from your mistakes.

Celebrate your successes: Recognize and celebrate your achievements, no matter how small they may be. This will help build your confidence and encourage you to take even more risks in the future.

## **Confidence:**

Identify and celebrate your strengths: Make a list of your accomplishments and strengths, and remind yourself of them regularly.

Face your fears: Identify the things that make you uncomfortable or fearful, and try to confront them one at a time.

Practice positive self-talk: Replace negative thoughts with positive affirmations, and remind yourself of your worth and abilities.

Set small goals and achieve them: Break down larger goals into smaller, achievable steps, and celebrate your progress along the way.

Get out of your comfort zone: Try new things and challenge yourself to step outside of your comfort zone on a regular basis.

Surround yourself with positive people: Spend time with people who uplift and support you, and avoid those who bring you down.

Take care of your physical health: Exercise regularly, eat well, and get enough rest to help you feel your best.

Practice good posture and body language: Stand tall, make eye contact, and speak clearly to convey confidence.

Develop a growth mindset: Embrace challenges and failures as opportunities to learn and grow, rather than setbacks.

Practice mindfulness and self-reflection: Take time to reflect on your thoughts and feelings, and practice mindfulness techniques like meditation to help you stay centered and focused.

## Time Management:

Identify your goals and priorities: Determine what is most important to you and prioritize your tasks accordingly.

Make a schedule: Create a daily or weekly schedule to help you manage your time more effectively.

Use a planner or to-do list: Write down your tasks and deadlines in a planner or to-do list to help you stay organized and on track.

Break down larger tasks: Break down larger tasks into smaller, more manageable tasks to make them feel less overwhelming.

Set deadlines: Set realistic deadlines for each task to help you stay focused and motivated.

Minimize distractions: Avoid distractions such as social media, email, or other non-work-related activities during your work time.

Take breaks: Take regular breaks to recharge and avoid burnout.

Delegate tasks: If possible, delegate tasks to others to help you manage your workload more effectively.

Learn to say no: Don't overcommit yourself by taking on too many tasks. Learn to say no to requests that don't align with your goals and priorities.

Review and adjust: Regularly review your progress and adjust your schedule and priorities as needed to help you stay on track and achieve your goals.

## **Leadership:**

Identify your leadership style: There are several types of leadership styles, such as autocratic, democratic, transformational, and servant leadership. Identify which style aligns best with your personality and values.

Set goals: Identify specific leadership goals you want to achieve, such as improving communication with team members or developing a more inclusive team environment.

Build self-awareness: Understand your strengths and weaknesses as a leader. This can be done through self-reflection, feedback from others, or assessments like personality tests.

Develop emotional intelligence: Emotional intelligence involves being aware of and managing your emotions, as well as understanding and empathizing with the emotions of others. Focus on developing this skill to become a more effective leader.

Communicate effectively: Practice active listening and clear communication to ensure that team members understand expectations, goals, and feedback.

Build relationships: Develop positive relationships with team members and other stakeholders. This involves being approachable, trustworthy, and demonstrating empathy.

Develop decision-making skills: Leaders must make tough decisions. Develop skills in gathering information, considering alternatives, and making informed decisions.

Learn to delegate: Effective leaders know how to delegate tasks to team members and empower them to take ownership of their work.

Develop conflict resolution skills: Conflict is inevitable in any group, but leaders must be able to handle it effectively.

Learn techniques for conflict resolution and practice them regularly.

Continuously learn: The best leaders never stop learning. Seek out opportunities for professional development, networking, and mentorship to continue to grow as a leader.

## **<u>Humility:</u>**

Practice self-reflection: Take time to reflect on your thoughts, actions, and behaviors. Be honest with yourself and identify areas where you may be lacking humility.

Seek feedback: Ask others for feedback on your behavior and actions. Listen to their feedback without becoming defensive and use it to improve.

Learn from others: Humble people recognize that they don't know everything and can learn from others. Seek out opportunities to learn from people with different perspectives and experiences.

Embrace imperfection: Accept that you are not perfect and that you will make mistakes. Recognize that mistakes can be opportunities for growth and learning.

Avoid judgment: Refrain from judging others and instead seek to understand their perspective. Everyone has a different story and journey, and humility requires us to recognize that.

Serve others: Focus on serving others rather than being served. Look for opportunities to help others and put their needs before your own.

Practice gratitude: Cultivate a sense of gratitude for what you have and the people in your life. Recognize that you wouldn't be where you are without the help and support of others.

Stay teachable: Stay open to new ideas and ways of doing things. Don't get stuck in your ways and be willing to adapt to changing circumstances.

Acknowledge your limitations: Recognize that you have limitations and that you can't do everything alone. Seek out help and support when you need it.

Practice humility daily: Make a conscious effort to practice humility every day. It takes time and effort to develop humility, so make it a priority in your life.

## **Self Awareness:**

Set aside time for self-reflection: Schedule some time each day or week to reflect on your thoughts, feelings, and behaviors. This can be through meditation, journaling, or simply sitting quietly and thinking.

Seek feedback: Ask others for honest feedback on your strengths and weaknesses. This can be from friends, family, coworkers, or a coach/mentor.

Identify your triggers: Pay attention to what triggers certain emotions or behaviors in you. This can help you become more aware of your reactions and learn to manage them more effectively.

Practice mindfulness: Mindfulness is the practice of being present and fully engaged in the moment. This can help you become more aware of your thoughts and feelings as they arise.

Use self-assessment tools: There are many self-assessment tools available online that can help you gain a better understanding of your personality, values, and strengths.

Challenge your assumptions: Question your beliefs and assumptions about yourself and the world around you. This can help you become more open-minded and empathetic towards others.

Embrace your imperfections: Accept that you are not perfect and that everyone makes mistakes. This can help you become more self-compassionate and less self-critical.

Reflect on your goals and values: Spend some time thinking about what is truly important to you and what you want to achieve in life. This can help you align your actions with your values and live a more fulfilling life.

Learn from your experiences: Reflect on past experiences and what you have learned from them. This can help you identify patterns in your behavior and make more informed decisions in the future.

Practice self-care: Take care of your physical, emotional, and mental health. This can help you become more aware of your needs and become more resilient in the face of challenges.

## **Curiosity:**

Cultivate an open mind: Be open to new experiences and ideas.

Ask questions: Ask questions about things that interest you and seek out answers.

Read and learn: Read books, and articles, and watch videos on topics that intrigue you.

Explore your interests: Pursue hobbies and interests that excite you.

Challenge assumptions: Don't take things at face value, challenge assumptions and investigate.

Experiment and try new things: Be willing to try new things and experiment to see what works for you.

Embrace failure: Don't be afraid to fail, use it as an opportunity to learn and improve.

Network and collaborate: Connect with people who share your interests and collaborate on projects.

Travel and experience new cultures: Travel to new places and experience new cultures to broaden your perspective.

Practice mindfulness: Practice being present in the moment, observe your surroundings and be curious about what you see.

## Communication:

Start by listening actively: Pay attention to the person speaking, ask questions, and avoid interrupting them.

Be aware of your body language: Your body language can affect the message you are trying to convey. Maintain eye contact, keep your posture straight, and avoid fidgeting.

Use clear and concise language: Speak in a way that is easy to understand, using simple words and avoiding jargon.

Practice speaking in public: Find opportunities to speak in front of others, such as presenting at work, joining a public speaking group, or volunteering to speak at an event.

Use the right tone of voice: Match the tone of your voice to the message you are trying to convey. For example, if you are speaking about a serious topic, use a serious tone of voice.

Practice active listening: Repeat what the other person said to confirm your understanding of the message and demonstrate that you are actively engaged in the conversation.

Use positive language: Focus on the positive and avoid using negative language or criticism.

Be aware of cultural differences: Different cultures have different communication styles, so be aware of cultural differences and adapt your communication style accordingly.

Use feedback: Ask for feedback from others to improve your communication skills and identify areas that need improvement.

Practice, practice, practice: Like any skill, communication requires practice. Make an effort to communicate effectively in all aspects of your life, and seek out opportunities to improve your communication skills.

## **Gratitude:**

Start a gratitude journal: Write down three things you are grateful for each day. This can help you focus on the positive aspects of your life and cultivate a grateful mindset.

Practice mindfulness: Pay attention to the present moment and notice the things around you that you are grateful for. This can be as simple as feeling the warmth of the sun on your skin or appreciating the beauty of a flower.

Express gratitude to others: Tell the people in your life that you appreciate them and what they do for you. This can help strengthen relationships and build a sense of community.

Give back: Volunteer your time or resources to help those in need. This can help you appreciate what you have and feel a sense of purpose.

Reframe negative thoughts: Instead of focusing on what you don't have, try to reframe your thoughts to focus on what you do have. This can help shift your mindset towards gratitude.

Practice empathy: Try to put yourself in other people's shoes and understand their perspectives. This can help you appreciate the people in your life and the challenges they may be facing.

Focus on the little things: Sometimes the smallest things can bring us the most joy. Try to appreciate the small moments and simple pleasures in life.

Take care of yourself: Practicing self-care can help you feel grateful for your body, mind, and overall well-being.

Surround yourself with positivity: Spend time with people who lift you up and inspire you. This can help you maintain a positive mindset and appreciate the good things in your life.

Practice gratitude daily: Make gratitude a part of your daily routine, whether it's through journaling, meditation, or simply taking a few moments to reflect on what you're thankful for.

## **Knowing Oneself:**

Practice mindfulness: Start by observing your thoughts, emotions, and physical sensations without judging them. Mindfulness helps you become more aware of your inner experiences and develop a deeper understanding of yourself.

Reflect on your values: Think about what is important to you and what values guide your life. This can help you understand your priorities and what motivates you.

Explore your interests: Engage in activities that interest you and bring you joy. This can help you discover your passions and what you enjoy doing.

Assess your strengths and weaknesses: Take an honest look at your strengths and weaknesses. This can help you understand what you excel at and what areas you need to work on.

Identify your personality traits: Take personality assessments or reflect on your personality traits. This can help you understand why you behave in certain ways and how you relate to others.

Examine your past experiences: Reflect on your past experiences and how they have shaped you. This can help you understand your beliefs and behaviors.

Seek feedback: Ask trusted friends or family members for feedback on your strengths and areas for improvement. This can provide an outside perspective on how you come across to others.

Journal: Write down your thoughts, feelings, and experiences in a journal. This can help you process your emotions and gain insights into yourself.

Practice self-compassion: Be kind and compassionate to yourself, just as you would be to a friend. This can help you develop a more positive relationship with yourself.

Seek therapy: Consider seeing a therapist or counselor to work through any issues that may be blocking your self-awareness. A trained professional can help you gain deeper insights into yourself and work through any emotional or psychological barriers.